To Sebastian, Izzie, Daisy, Johnny and Delphina,
and Natsue, Ferdinand and Takae,
children of my heart, with all my love
—Danie ♥ Danielle

For my Jovie.
May you know how deeply you're loved.
—K.V.

Text copyright © 2014 by Danielle Steel
Jacket art and interior illustrations copyright © 2014 by Kristi Valiant
Jacket and book design by Jan Gerardi

All rights reserved. Published in the United States by Doubleday, an imprint of Random House Children's Books,
a division of Random House LLC, a Penguin Random House Company, New York.

Doubleday and the colophon are registered trademarks of Random House LLC.

Visit us on the Web! randomhouse.com/kids

Educators and librarians, for a variety of teaching tools,
visit us at RHTeachersLibrarians.com

Library of Congress Cataloging-in-Publication Data
Steel, Danielle.
Pretty Minnie in Paris / by Danielle Steel ; illustrated by Kristi Valiant. — First edition.
pages cm.
Summary: In Paris, France, Minnie, a long-haired teacup chihuahua who loves to dress up, gets separated from her
fashion-loving owner, Francoise, at a fashion show.
ISBN 978-0-385-37000-4 (trade) — ISBN 978-0-375-97182-2 (lib. bdg.) —
ISBN 978-0-375-98167-8 (ebook)
[1. Chihuahua (Dog breed)—Fiction. 2. Dogs—Fiction. 3. Fashion—Fiction. 4. Fashion shows—Fiction.
5. Paris (France)—Fiction. 6. France—Fiction.] I. Valiant, Kristi, illustrator. II. Title.
PZ7.S8143Pre 2014 [E]—dc23 2013015050

MANUFACTURED IN CHINA
10 9 8 7 6 5 4 3 2 1
First Edition

DANIELLE STEEL

Pretty Minnie
in Paris

illustrated
by Kristi Valiant

DOUBLEDAY BOOKS FOR YOUNG READERS

Minnie is a white, long-haired,
teacup-size Chihuahua.

She **loves** to wear shoes.

Minnie belongs to Françoise.
They live in Paris near the
Arc de Triomphe.

Françoise takes Minnie
everywhere with her,
except to school.

They like to go to the top
of the Eiffel Tower,

go to their favorite
bistro for lunch,

and ride their bicycle in the
Jardin du Luxembourg.

Françoise likes pretty clothes. She likes pink and purple and things that sparkle. Minnie does too. She has the perfect outfit for every occasion.

Here's what Minnie hates: her snowsuit.

When Françoise puts it on her, Minnie rolls over with her legs straight up in the air like a beetle on its back, and refuses to get up until Françoise takes it off.

Françoise's mother designs beautiful clothes. Françoise and Minnie love to visit the workrooms where hats and dresses, evening gowns, and fancy shoes are made.

Minnie likes to be helpful.

Minnie and Françoise love the fashion shows best
of all. The clothes are beautiful, and there are lots
of people, lots of photographers, and lots of noise.

But the first time Minnie went to a fashion
show, there was so much excitement and
so many people that she got scared.

Minnie jumped off Françoise's lap, and when
no one was looking she ran behind the curtain
to the dressing room backstage.

Françoise didn't know where Minnie was. The show
had started and she couldn't leave her seat to look for
her. Françoise was scared. What if Minnie ran away
and was really lost? She started to cry.

Françoise wasn't having any fun.

Minnie wasn't having any fun either.
All she wanted was to find Françoise and go home.

Suddenly, Minnie saw the last
model come down the runway in
a wedding dress. Minnie barked.

Everyone watched as the model smiled and stopped and picked Minnie up. The model held her in one hand with her bouquet. Minnie wondered where they were going, and hoped it was back to Françoise.

When Françoise saw Minnie, she jumped out of her seat and clapped. Just then, a photographer ran up and took a picture of the model holding Minnie. Françoise rushed over and took Minnie in her arms.

Minnie put her paws around Françoise's neck and licked her face. She was so happy she wasn't lost anymore.

After the show, Françoise told her mother what had happened—and she was happy to see Minnie too.

On the way home, Françoise and her mother and Minnie stopped at their favorite bistro for dinner to celebrate their big night.

As soon as they got home, Minnie climbed into her
fancy bed that Françoise's grandmother had made for
her. Minnie was so exhausted after her big adventure
that she went right to sleep.

The next day, there was a picture of Minnie in the newspaper. "You're famous!" Françoise said.

Minnie barked.

Minnie was the star of the show. But best
of all, she was the dog that Françoise loved
with all her heart.